Caroline Bi—————————————————————————ical College.

She has —————————————————————————erb artist,

special —————————————————————————l reality

that we c—————————————————————————or *Hue Boy*,

writte—————————————————————————s Prize.

As well—————————————————————————s written

a—————————————————————————*ft,*

'Saint' Merryn
1981~1997

—————

For Ray, William
and Johnny Dollar

Since Dad Left copyright © Frances Lincoln Limited 1998
Text and illustrations copyright © Caroline Binch 1998

First published in Great Britain in 1998 by Frances Lincoln Children's Books,
4 Torriano Mews, Torriano Avenue, London NW5 2RZ

www.franceslincoln.com

First paperback edition 1999

British Library Cataloguing in Publication Data
available on request

ISBN: 978-0-7112-1355-5

Set in Stone Serif

Printed in Dongguan, Guangdon, China by Kwong Fat Offset Printing in December 2010

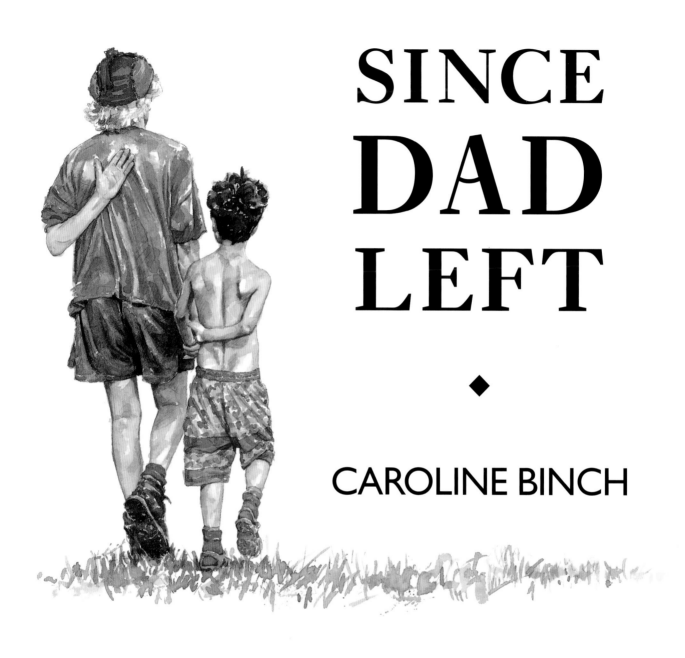

SINCE
DAD
LEFT

◆

CAROLINE BINCH

F

FRANCES LINCOLN
CHILDREN'S BOOKS

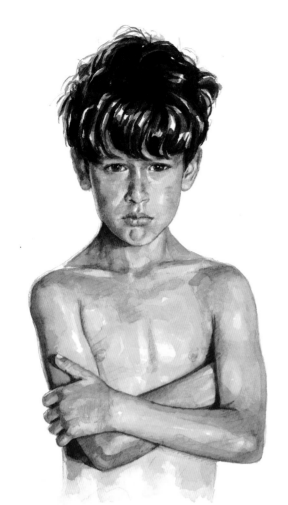

Sid was cross. He often felt cross, now that his mum and dad didn't live together any more.

He still had his dogs, of course - Doggo and Digger, plus the three cats, Kitty Mama, Marmite and Bertha. And most important of all - Sandra, his mum.

"It just wasn't working out with Dad and me together," said mum. "We were both unhappy."

Sid didn't understand. He thought they were more unhappy now.

Most days, Sid had school to think about. He liked to get up early in the morning and eat a big bowl of cereal in the kitchen. Then he and his mum walked down the path to wait for the school bus.

Sid felt very grown-up paying for his ticket and going off to school on his own. His friends caught the same bus and there was always lots to talk about. But since Dad left, there were times when he just wanted to sit on his own and look out of the window at the fields and sky floating by.

At school, Sid liked art best of all.
He loved to paint skies with
rockets and moons and stars.
Sid drew brilliant rockets.

"One day, I'm going to fly far away with Doggo and Digger
and find an amazing planet where everyone is happy,"
Sid told his friends. They all wanted to come with him,
but Sid knew there wouldn't be enough food and oxygen
for everyone - just enough for him, Mum and Dad, Doggo
and Digger and the cats.

After school, the bus brought Sid home and he ate his tea
with Mum, watching television.

Now Dad wasn't there, Doggo and Digger were allowed to snuggle up with him.

Sometimes Josh and Ben came to play. Their favourite game was hide-and-seek, because Sid's house had lots of good places to hide.

Since Dad left, Sid had tried to stay lost, even after the game was over. He felt safe, tucked away in a secret place where no one could find him.

One Saturday, Sid was extra cross. He trod on Doggo's tail and didn't care when the dog yelped.

"I don't want to see Mick," said Sid angrily. "I don't like him. He went away."

"He's your dad, Sid. And it's only for one day," Mum said. "He misses you a lot. It isn't all his fault."

"He's not my dad any more!" said Sid, scowling, "and I don't want to go."

But his mum insisted. She drove Sid the few miles to where Mick was living, near Grandad's house.

When he saw Mick, Sid didn't know what to do.
He decided not to say a word. Sandra and Mick
didn't speak to each other, so why should he?

Mick didn't seem to notice that Sid wasn't talking,
or that he had on his fiercest 'hate you' face.

"It's great to see you, Sid. I've thought of lots of
things for us to do," said Mick. He patted and fussed
over the dogs, who were overjoyed to see him.

Traitors, thought Sid. Dogs swapped sides
far too easily.

"I've just got to milk the goats, Sid, then I'll show
you what I've been doing since I last saw you."

Sid was dying to say, "Don't care," in his
nastiest voice. He sat down and pretended
not to see or hear Mick, the goats,
or those stupid dogs.

"Look, Sid," said Mick. "This is my new house."

"That's not a house – you can't live there!" The words jumped out of Sid's mouth before he could stop them.

"Oh, a bender may look strange," said Mick, smiling. "But it's better than most houses, I can tell you. Come and see."

Sid followed Mick inside. He saw a woodburner, a cooker,
a big bed and a little bed.

"Try the bed," said Mick.
Sid tried it, reluctantly.

"It's hard. I'm not sleeping
here, ever," said Sid.

He jumped down and walked
outside. He was so surprised by
Mick's new home, he'd forgotten
that he wasn't speaking to him!

"Well, any time you change
your mind, it's here for you,"
said Mick. "Doggo and Digger
seem to like it."

Mick picked up a rucksack.

"I've got some bread and cheese in here, so we can go for a ride with Oliver and the cart," he said.

Mick had been promising to fix up the cart for as long as Sid could remember. Now it was newly painted in bright colours.

While Mick was harnessing Oliver to the cart, Sid gave the horse some carrots. He loved how Oliver's big soft, bristly mouth trembled against his hand.

He had been missing Oliver a lot.

Out in the narrow lanes, Oliver's hooves clipped and clopped, his big tail swished at flies and his ears twitched. Sid started to feel better. If only his mum could be here too!

It was hot. Mick took Oliver through an old gate and into a wood, where the track stopped by a lake.

"Well, I'm going for a swim," said Mick. "You coming, Sid?"

Sid felt silly sitting in the cart while Oliver munched grass and Mick and the dogs enjoyed the water.

"I'll just have a paddle," said Sid. He stepped carefully through the squishy mud at the edge of the lake.

It felt so good in the water
that Sid forgot to be cross.
It was just like old times.

Late in the afternoon they got back
to the bender, put Oliver in his field and
fed the dogs. Mick started making supper.
Sid was tired. He climbed up into a tree where
he could watch Mick.

"I'd love you to stay and sleep in the bender tonight, Sid," said Mick, "but if you want to go home, that's fine. I'm lighting a fire later, because some friends are coming."
Sid didn't answer.
He wanted to stay - but he wanted to go to his mum.

Mick's friends arrived in high spirits. They sat around the fire, eating under the stars. One of them, Sean, told scary ghost stories especially for Sid. They played music on drums, a trumpet and long didgeree-doos, which made funny burpy sounds that made Sid laugh. They sang, too - fast songs that they all clapped to, then some soft songs that made Sid feel sad. Mum had a beautiful voice, but she hadn't sung since Dad left.

Sid sighed, and fell asleep between Mick, Doggo and Digger. The last thing he remembered was Mick tucking him up in bed.

"Yes, I want to stay tonight, Dad," he said sleepily.

Mick kissed his forehead. "I'm very happy to have you here. Sleep tight."

The singing and laughing outside warmed Sid's dreams.

Next morning, Sid went outside and found Mick having a cup of tea.

"Hi, Sid," said Mick. "I've milked the goats. Want some milk?"

Sid said nothing. Mick came and sat by him with a cup of milk.

"Look, Sid, I feel really bad about your mum, and breaking up and hurting you. But we both love you. It would be good if you would come every weekend. See how you feel later on. It's time to meet Mum now."

Sid felt muddled. He wanted to hit Mick as hard as he could - but give him a big hug at the same time.

Then he saw his mum,
and ran off across the field,
shouting to her. It must
have been the wind that
made his eyes water.

"Hello, my wonderful boy,"
said Mum. "I'm so happy to
see you." Her smile made
Sid feel like smiling too.
He looked back and saw
Mick still watching.

"Bye, Dad!" he shouted.
"See you soon."

MORE TITLES FROM FRANCES LINCOLN CHILDREN'S BOOKS

Christy's Dream
Caroline Binch

Christy has wanted a pony for as long as he can remember.
Lots of other boys on the estate have their own horses,
so now Christy's saved up enough money no-one can stop him
making his dream come true. Except his ma. What will she say
when he brings his new horse home?

Silver Shoes
Caroline Binch

Molly loves to dance, and she desperately wants some
silver shoes to wear to her first dance class. But her mum says
she has to wait and see if she likes the classes first. Nearly all
the other girls are wearing silver shoes, even Molly's best friend!

Petar's Song
Pratima Mitchell
Illustrated by Caroline Binch

Petar loves music and the tunes he plays on his violin
keep everyone in the village dancing. But when war breaks out
Petar, his mother, brother and sister have to leave their valley
and cross the border to safety leaving their father behind.
So badly does Petar miss his father that he cannot play his violin –
until one day a song of peace comes into his head...

Frances Lincoln titles are available from all good bookshops.
You can also buy books and find out more about your favourite titles,
authors and illustrators on our website: www.franceslincoln.com